I Love Blue

by Andra Cloud-Flowers
Pictures by Christopher Jeckering

DORRANCE
PUBLISHING CO
EST. 1920
PITTSBURGH, PENNSYLVANIA 15238

The contents of this work, including, but not limited to, the accuracy of events, people, and places depicted; opinions expressed; permission to use previously published materials included; and any advice given or actions advocated are solely the responsibility of the author, who assumes all liability for said work and indemnifies the publisher against any claims stemming from publication of the work.

Dorrance Publishing Co
585 Alpha Drive
Suite 103
Pittsburgh, PA 15238
Visit our website at *www.dorrancebookstore.com*

ISBN: 978-1-6470-2211-2
eISBN: 978-1-6470-2912-8

I Love Blue

When I have breakfast in the morning, Blue is with me.

Can you see Blue?
Blue is always with me.

After eating,
we play with toys.

On special days,
Granny takes Blue and me
to my school.

I have been going to my school for a long time.

All the people
at my school know
Granny, me, and Blue.

When we come in,
they say hello to all of us.

Then Granny walks me to
my class and says goodbye.

That's when it is time for
Blue and I to go inside.

Blue loves to read with Granny and me in the big brown rocking chair

Some nights Granny says
Blue needs to take a bath
and get squeaky clean,

but Blue is always waiting
for me at bedtime.

On weekends Granny and I visit family. I keep Blue with me for the ride.

If I am feeling scared,
Blue helps me feel brave.

Granny and I talk about the new school I will go to soon.

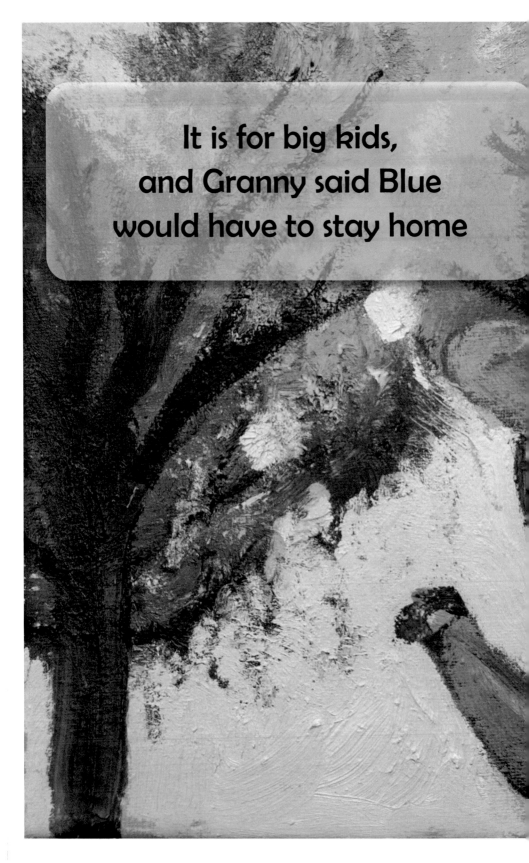

It is for big kids,
and Granny said Blue
would have to stay home

when it is time
for me to start my new
school in the fall.

I think Granny is silly
when she says that,

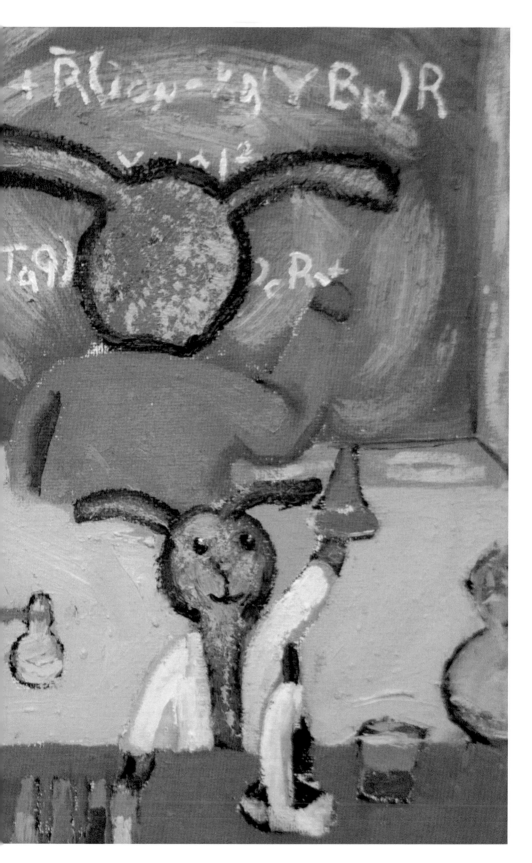

but I guess we will find out.
I love Blue.